For our parents,
Stephen and Cheryl Brabham
Thank you for the frequent trips to the library.

For our grandmothers,
Norma L. Morton and Francis E. McKissick
Thank you for the childhood memories
which inspire us to write.

A.S.B

Copyright 2019 by Adijah & Atiya Brabham
All rights reserved. No part of this book may be reproduced
or transmitted in any form or by any mean, electronic or mechanical,
including photocopying, recording, or by any information storage
and retrieval system without permission in writing from the publisher.

For information regarding permission, write to:

PrairieClover Publishing Company
176-25 Union Turnpike Suite 391
Fresh Meadows, New York, 11366
Info@prairiecloverpublishing.com

Library of Congress Cataloging-in Publication Data Available

ISBN: 978-0578-56386-2
First Edition: 2019

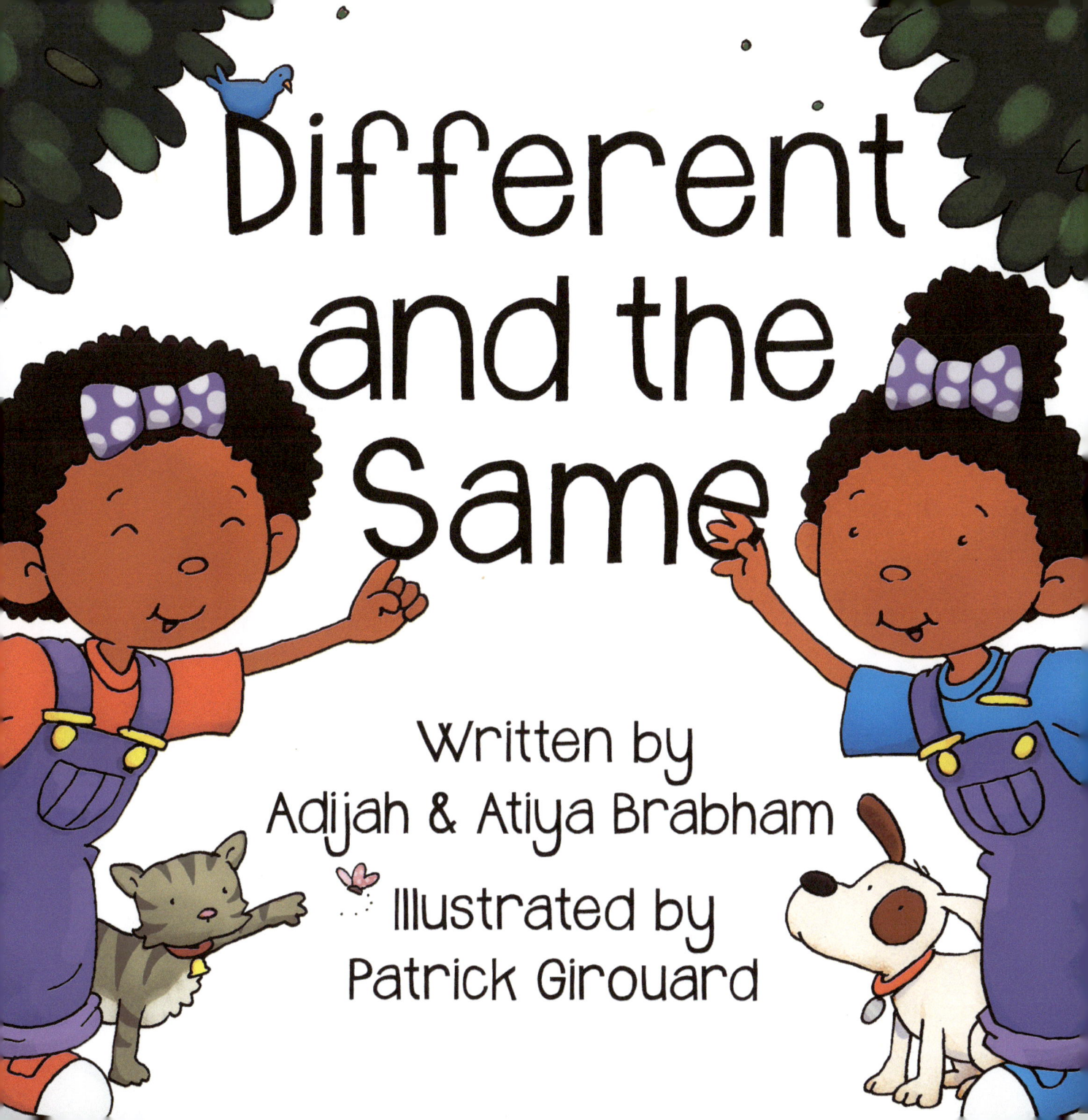

Nia and Nori are sisters.
They have the same eyes,
mouth, ears, and nose.
They are identical twins,
I suppose.

Nori loves her puffy ponytail.

Nia loves her curly afro.

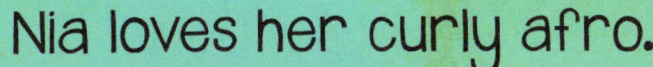

They both like to wear BIG polka dot bows.

They are different and the same you see...

Nia likes to eat vegetable pie.

They both enjoy helping grandma cook,

It's a fun thing to do!
They are different and the same you see...

Nia's favorite pets are cats.

Nori's favorite pets are dogs.

Nia loves to splash and swim.

They both like to climb the jungle gym.

They are different and the same you see...

Nia is an architect.

Nori is an engineer.

They both work together to build TALL skyscrapers, far and near.

They both like to feed the animals and take pictures too!

They are different and the same you see...

Nia's favorite color is red.

They both like to experiment to make something new!

They are different and the same you see...

Nia likes to sing and draw.

Nori likes to write.

CPSIA information can be obtained
at www.ICGtesting.com
Printed in the USA
BVHW020349091119
563253BV00001BA/1/P